LEGENDS
HEROES AND VILLAINS

Also by Anthony Horowitz from
Macmillan Children's Books

LEGENDS: BATTLES AND QUESTS

LEGENDS: BEASTS AND MONSTERS

LEGENDS: DEATH AND THE UNDERWORLD

LEGENDS: THE WRATH OF THE GODS

LEGENDS: TRICKS AND TRANSFORMATIONS

LEGENDS

ANTHONY HOROWITZ

HEROES AND VILLAINS

Illustrated by Thomas Yeates

MACMILLAN CHILDREN'S BOOKS

First published 2011 by Macmillan Children's Books

This edition published 2013 by Macmillan Children's Books
a division of Macmillan Publishers Limited
20 New Wharf Road, London N1 9RR
Basingstoke and Oxford
Associated companies throughout the world
www.panmacmillan.com

ISBN 978-1-4472-5472-0

1 3 5 7 9 8 6 4 2

A CIP catalogue record for this book is available from
the British Library.

Printed and bound by CPI Group (UK) Ltd, Croydon, CR0 4YY

CONTENTS

INTRODUCTION

One question I'm often asked is: 'Who is your hero?' It's not an easy question to answer. Do you mean living or dead, real or fictitious? And what exactly *is* a hero?

My heroes include Charles Dickens, the greatest writer who ever lived, Winston Churchill, Ernest Shackleton, who survived brutal conditions trapped at the South Pole and led all his men to safety, Aung San Suu Kyi, who has spent her entire life fighting for democracy in Burma and, surprisingly, David Beckham, one of the few footballers who doesn't seem to be totally unpleasant. I have a few fictitious heroes too: Flashman (who actually isn't very heroic at all), Tintin and James Bond.

Even a quick glance at this list shows how very different heroes can be – and I think this is true of myths and legends too. Gawain is a hero in English legend more because of what he doesn't do than because of what he does.

Achilles, in Greek mythology, is argumentative, angry and cruel. What are we to make of the small and ugly Maui who turns up in a rather odd Polynesian story and battles it out with the sun? The truth is that it's hard to think of any hero in any myth or legend who is faultless . . . and if they were, they'd probably be insufferable.

All in all, villains are much more fun. (That great writer Milton discovered this when he wrote *Paradise Lost*. Satan is a fantastic character, full of darkness and energy. God and the angels are all much less interesting). I loved writing about the bloodthirsty Grendel. I couldn't imagine why Procrustes killed travellers in quite such an unpleasant way, but I enjoyed trying to figure it out. And I have to admit that in many respects I found Hercules rather dull and much preferred writing about his enemy, the feeble King Eurystheus.

The same is true about my Alex Rider books, by the way – what makes Alex so attractive is that he doesn't *want* to be a hero. He's very much forced into his missions against his will. And my favourite characters in the books are always the bad guys with their various insane schemes to blow up the world or whatever. In fact, when I'm writing the books, that's where I always start. Think about it for a minute. Where would Batman be without the Joker? How could you have Robin Hood without the Sheriff of Nottingham? At the end of the day, heroes and villains are inextricably linked. You simply can't have one without the other.

One other thing I want to mention in this introduction. I have been at great pains to point out that these versions of the myths and legends are not new . . . in fact I wrote them thirty years ago. That said, the longest entry in this collection, my version of 'Gawain and the Green Knight', was commissioned specially for this edition and appears for the first time. The excellent illustrations by Thomas Yeates are also new, as are the glossy covers. So if you like myths and legends as much as I do, I hope this is a book you will enjoy.

Anthony Horowitz

THE EYE OF THE CYCLOPS

Greek

The Eye of the Cyclops

The Cyclops was certainly a terrifying creature. It was about the height of a two-storey house with thick, curly hair, a matted (and usually filthy) beard and only one eye, set square in the middle of its forehead. It was grotesquely ugly, extremely bad-tempered, inordinately violent and generally worth going a long way to avoid. All this, any good book of Greek myths will tell you. But what is less often mentioned is the fact that the Cyclops was also incredibly stupid. It was probably one of the most stupid monsters that ever lived.

There were a great many Cyclopes. At one time they had been employed as blacksmiths for Zeus but after a while they had forgotten not only how to do the work but what the work was that they were supposed to do, and had become shepherds instead. They were shepherds for almost two hundred years before it occurred to them to go and buy some sheep. Then they took their sheep and settled on an island in the middle of the

Aegean Sea where they lived in caves, seldom if ever talking to one another. There were two reasons for this. The first was that the Cyclopes were poor conversationalists, often forgetting the beginning of a sentence when they were only halfway through. But also, if there was one thing a Cyclops couldn't stand, it was another Cyclops.

The most famous Cyclops was called Polyphemus. He was the son of Poseidon, the god of the sea, but preferred to stay very much on land, looking after a flock of sheep. Polyphemus had no friends but was on intimate terms with most of the sheep. He knew them all by name, chatted to them, milked them as gently as his huge fingers could manage and shed real tears whenever he had to slaughter one in order to make his particularly delicious lamb stew.

One day, returning to his cave after a hard day's work in the hills, he was astonished to find that he had had visitors. They were still there in fact, sitting in front of his fire and feasting on one of his sheep. There were about a dozen of them and, looking more closely, he was delighted to see that they were human beings.

Polyphemus loved human beings in his own way . . . which was cooked or raw. What he particularly liked about them was the way their bones crunched between his teeth but never got caught in his throat.

The giant's face lit up in a great smile. It was also a horrible smile for, having just one

eye in the middle of his forehead, everything he did with his face was rather horrible.

'Who are you?' he demanded.

The men had by now huddled together and were looking up at him with a mixture of horror and terror. Then one of them stepped forward.

'Good monster,' he said, 'we are Greeks. We are returning home having fought a great war at Troy. We stopped here to find fresh provisions for our ship and thought to pass the night in your cave.'

Polyphemus scowled. He had never heard of Troy and didn't particularly like being addressed as 'monster'.

The man bowed low. 'I am sure you need no reminding,' he said, 'of the laws of Zeus, which demand hospitality to poor travellers such as ourselves. And I . . .'

But he was wasting his time. Polyphemus didn't even know what 'hospitality' meant. Moreover, he was hungry. His mouth had been watering from the moment he had seen the human beings. Now, brushing the man aside, he grabbed two of his companions by their feet, dashed their brains out on the stone floor and tossed them into his mouth. Crunch! Crunch! He shivered with pleasure as they slid down his throat. Two men from twelve left nine (or was it eleven?) and if he had two more for breakfast and two more for dinner every day, they would last him until . . .

But the mathematical sum was too difficult for him. Rolling a huge stone in front of the cave's exit, he fell into a contented sleep.

He would have slept less well if he had known just who the men in the cave were. They were, as their leader had said, Greek warriors returning home from the ten long years of war that had raged around the city of Troy, and which had only ended with the famous trick of the Trojan Horse. Their leader was called Odysseus and he was to become one of the most celebrated of the Greek heroes.

He was a king, the King of Ithaca. It was Odysseus who often claimed the credit for the invention of the wooden horse, although it had in fact been the idea of Athene, the goddess of wisdom. But it was certainly true that Odysseus had been one of the men who had hidden inside the horse and he had fought most valiantly in the sack of Troy. And whether he invented the wooden horse or not, he was well-known for his cunning and trickery.

There seemed little he could do in his present predicament, however. The stone that Polyphemus had rolled across the entrance to the cave was far too big to move and it fitted exactly without any cracks to slip through. The following morning, when the giant woke up, he could only watch helplessly as two more of his men were seized and devoured. Then the giant left, herding his sheep in front of him, and at last Odysseus was able to set his mind to work.

It was often cold on the island and Polyphemus kept a plentiful supply of wood for his fire. Each log was the size of a small tree – indeed, that's just what many of them were, for the Cyclops often plucked up whole trees and carried them home. Odysseus ordered his men to draw their swords and together they began hacking at one of the logs. It took them hours, but by the time evening arrived, they had removed all the branches, cut the tip to a needle-sharp point and hidden the whole thing at the back of the cave.

Then the stone rolled aside, the sheep came in and behind them Polyphemus. Two more of the unfortunate travellers found themselves lifted into the air, screamed as their skulls were cracked and disappeared into the giant's mouth. But this time, before Polyphemus could fall asleep, Odysseus approached him.

'Sweet monster,' he cried, 'I hope you have enjoyed my two friends.'

'They were a bit chewy,' Polyphemus replied.

'That was probably their armour. But I was wondering, dear giant, if you would care to quench your thirst with some wine after your delicious supper?'

'What's wine?' the Cyclops asked.

'It is a drink made from grapes, O mighty one,' Odysseus explained. 'By chance, I have two barrels with me here. Please be my guest . . .'

He gestured towards the barrel which held enough wine for twenty men. Polyphemus snatched it up and downed the whole lot in one mouthful.

'It's good!' he exclaimed. 'Do you have more?'

'One more barrel, your greatness,' Odysseus said.

'Give it to me!'

'With pleasure.'

Polyphemus grabbed the second barrel and drank that one down too. But the wine was very strong and as the giant had never had alcohol before, it had an immediate effect on him. He became rather drunk.

'Washernem?' he asked.

'I beg your pardon?' Odysseus said.

'Your name? Wash your name?'

'It is Oudeis,' Odysseus told him, this being the Greek word for 'nobody'.

'Nobody?' Polyphemus repeated. 'Well . . . Nobody is my friend. And because he's my friend, I'll eat Nobody last of all. I'll eat all the others first. Then Nobody after.'

And with that, Polyphemus fell into a drunken slumber.

At once, Odysseus and his remaining comrades lifted up the log they had prepared and thrust the point into the fire. Soon

the tip was white-hot and crackling. The noise might have woken Polyphemus up, but because of the wine he was in a deep sleep and didn't even stir when Odysseus climbed on to his chest. But he woke up and screamed the place down when the six men drove the burning stake right into his eye, turning it round and leaving it jutting out of his forehead. The Greek warriors raced to the back of the cave as he leaped up and down bellowing so loudly that the walls shook and dust cascaded down. The noise was so great that several other Cyclopes gathered round the mouth of the cave and demanded to know what was the matter.

'I am blinded and in ghastly pain,' Polyphemus moaned.

'How did it happen?' one of the Cyclopes called out.

'It was Nobody's fault,' Polyphemus explained.

'You mean . . . it was an accident?'

'No! No! Nobody did it to me. I blame

Nobody. And I'm going to kill Nobody on account of it.'

The Cyclopes looked at one another and scratched their heads.

'If nobody's done anything,' they said at last, 'you must be having a bad dream. Why don't you just go back to sleep and leave us in peace?'

With that, they turned their backs on the cave and went back to bed.

The following morning found Polyphemus in a miserable state. There were no Greek soldiers for breakfast that day. He couldn't even manage a piece of toast or a boiled sheep. Everything was dark for him and he had a blinding headache. Nonetheless, he rolled the stone aside to let his flock out to pasture, taking great care to feel each animal with his hands in case any of the men tried to escape.

But this was what Odysseus had been waiting for. During the course of the night, he had tied some of the sheep together,

using their own long wool to do it. Then, in exactly the same way, he had tied his surviving friends underneath them so that they hung just above the ground. And although the blind giant ran his hands along the backs of the sheep, he didn't think to feel underneath them. So that way the Greeks were able to escape.

Odysseus was the last to leave. He had chosen the largest sheep for himself, not knowing that it was the giant's favourite. And to his dismay, he found himself stopped as the sheep reached the mouth of the cave.

'My dear Penelope,' Polyphemus sighed, addressing the sheep. 'Normally you're

the first to leave, but today you're the last. Could it be that you are upset because your master has been horribly hurt by Nobody?'

'Baaah!' Odysseus said.

'You run along then,' Polyphemus muttered, and, with Odysseus breathing a huge sigh of relief, he allowed the sheep to pass.

The escaped prisoners reached their ship and set sail as quickly as they could. As they left, Odysseus couldn't help laughing at the success of his plan and Polyphemus, hearing him, hurled a massive stone in the direction of the sound, missing the ship by inches.

Odysseus laughed again and called out to the giant.

'If anyone asks who blinded you, tell them it was Odysseus, son of Laertes and King of Ithaca. And perhaps the next time strangers call, you will remember the sacred laws of hospitality!'

But Polyphemus never showed anyone the slightest trace of hospitality. He spent the rest of his days sitting in the fields with his sheep, moaning to himself. And who can blame him? For it must be said that to lose one eye when you have two of them is a great misfortune, but if you have only one to begin with, then it is nothing short of a catastrophe.

THE ACHILLES HEEL

Greek

The Achilles Heel

This is the story of the greatest of all the Greek heroes. Achilles the fierce. Achilles the strong. Achilles the most courageous man who ever lived. It is also a story of that most terrible time in the history of Ancient Greece – about fourteen hundred years before the birth of Christ – when so many of its noblest princes were to fall in the ten long years of war at Troy.

You must imagine the city, vast and impregnable, its massive walls facing out towards a black, tormented sea. Overhead, the sky is thick with the smoke that pours out of the funeral pyres and from the forges where the blacksmiths work day and night, hammering at swords and shields, sharpening spears and arrowheads, fashioning the weapons of death. It is cold. A wind sweeps across the fields and a remorseless drizzle falls, stabbing at the pools that have formed in the mud, the water swirling round suddenly red as it mixes with the blood from the day's fighting.

Between the city of the Trojans and the tents of the Greeks nothing moves. Both sides are sleeping.

This is the scene that was to shape the legend of the life of Achilles. This was where he was to meet his death.

The Parents of Achilles

Achilles' mother was Thetis, a Nereid – one of the fifty nymphs of the sea who come to the aid of sailors – and an Immortal. His father was Peleus, King of the Myrmidons, but a mortal. The difference between the parents was to be the ruin of the marriage for Thetis had been forced to marry Peleus against her own wishes. There had been a time when Zeus had loved Thetis but she had coldly rejected him. In revenge, Zeus had decreed that she should never marry an Immortal, a command that had infuriated the proud Thetis.

'How can I live with a mere mortal?' she had cried. 'See what happens to mortal men with the passing of years. Their skin withers and their bellies sag. Their hair turns grey and their eyes become weak. No more can they run and fight. The passion within them grows cold. Am I to live with a decrepit, senile old man when I remain young and

beautiful? Am I to see my children grow old and die when I remain alive? It is unjust! It is an outrage!'

The marriage went ahead, but when her first child was born she stole it away and, holding it by the heel, dipped it in the chill water of the River Styx which winds its way through the Underworld. In this way did she make her child immortal. But she made one mistake, a mistake that was one day to prove fatal. For she forgot to immerse the heel itself and that part of the baby remained mortal.

When Peleus found out what his wife had done, he was furious. A mortal himself, he had wanted his son to grow up the same way. He therefore snatched the baby away – before Thetis had even had time to breast-feed it. For this reason, because his lips had never touched his mother's breast, the baby was called Achilles which means 'no lips'.

The Childhood of Achilles

Peleus and Thetis parted company immediately after this, Thetis returning to her home in the sea. Achilles was then entrusted to the care of Cheiron to be brought up amongst the olive trees on the slopes of Mount Pelion. Cheiron was a centaur, half-man and half-horse – but unlike many of the centaurs he was both gentle and wise.

Cheiron loved Achilles as though he were his own son. He fed the boy on the flesh of lions to give him courage and on sweet honeycombs to make him run swiftly. Who better was there to teach him how to ride and how to hunt? He also taught him the arts of pipe-playing and healing, and the immortal Calliope, one of the nine Muses, visited the cave to teach him how to sing. Soon Achilles had grown into a youth of extraordinary beauty as well as great skill. His body was broad-shouldered and muscular. His hair

tumbled down around his neck in a mass of golden curls. It is said that at the age of six he could outrun a full-grown stag and kill it with his own hands.

But while Achilles played in the sun on Mount Pelion, the clouds of war were gathering. It had been at the wedding of his own parents that Eris, goddess of discord, had sown the first seeds of disaster in the form of the golden apple that she had

presented 'to the fairest'. Already Paris had made his choice and stolen Helen away as his prize. And throughout Greece, warriors and princes were coming together, forming the great army that would soon sail to Troy.

Now Thetis had been given a prophecy. The prophecy stated simply that were Achilles to sail for Troy he would never return. Although she had allowed Peleus to steal her child, she was still devoted to him and now she hurried to Mount Pelion in an attempt to save him from his fate that was as vain as it was desperate. Dressing him up as a woman, she took him to the court of Lycomedes, King of Scyros, hoping that he would be able to hide there, safe from the searching eyes of the Greek kings.

Achilles goes to War

While Achilles wasted his days amongst the women of Scyros, the main protagonists of the Trojan war were coming together and travelling the country in search of warriors prepared to fight – and die – with them.

There was Menelaus, King of Sparta and the leader of the Greek forces. For Helen had been his wife and it had been his honour that had been assailed when Paris had stolen her. With him was Agamemnon, King of Mycenae, his brother. Nobody would fight more valiantly in the Trojan war. Nobody would die more treacherously after it. And there was Odysseus, who had himself feigned madness to try to avoid going to Troy and who would be condemned to wander for ten years before he saw his home again.

It was Odysseus who came to Scyros in search of Achilles, for a soothsayer had warned that Troy could not be taken without him. Faced with the bland smiles of the king and a palace that was filled – on the face of it – only with women, Odysseus was forced to resort to a trick. First he presented the women with a great heap of gifts; jewels, perfumes and beautiful dresses, but also

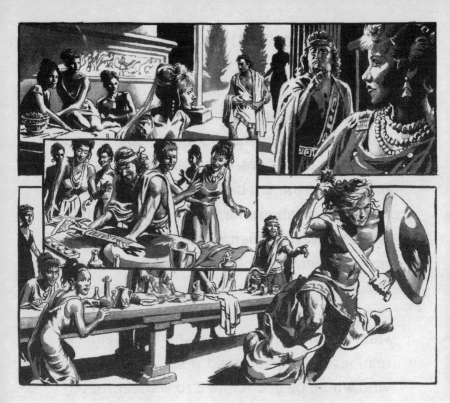

one sword and one shield. Then, while they argued over who got what, he gave the signal for his soldiers outside the palace to sound their trumpets and shout as if an army had just attacked. At once, one of the 'women' threw off her wig and seized the shield and sword and in this way was Achilles discovered and recruited to the army.

And so Achilles set out for Troy, taking

with him a magic spear that only he could wield – a gift from Cheiron – and also a chest inlaid with ivory and jewels and packed with blankets, tunics and cloaks to protect him against the wind – a present from his grieving mother. He was accompanied by his cousin, Patroclus, who was older than him but neither as skilful nor as well-born. Achilles loved him more than anyone else in the world.

Achilles at Troy

Achilles was the second Greek to leap on to the Trojan coast. He would have been the first had Thetis not warned him that the first to land would also be the first to die. This honour, if so it can be called, was taken by one Protesilaus who was promptly run through by Hector, the prince of Troy.

The first battle was fought on the beach and Achilles, leading his father's faithful Myrmidons, soon proved that he deserved his reputation for valour. In the heat of the fighting, he found himself confronted by Cycnus, the son of Poseidon and a ferocious warrior. In the first twenty minutes of the battle he had killed no fewer than a hundred Greeks and their blood coated every inch of his armour, and dripped out of his hair.

Achilles threw himself at him and the two fought furiously. Cycnus was more like a beast than a man, snarling in anger, his eyes wide with blood-lust. And he was seemingly invincible. Achilles would slash at him with his sword but either his opponent moved faster than the eye could see or the blade passed straight through him without so much as breaking his skin. He thrust his spear at him, but Cycnus caught the point in his bare hands and, with a horrible laugh, turned it aside.

At last Achilles managed to force him back, using the hilt of his sword to bludgeon him on the side of the head. Cycnus staggered and tripped over. At once, Achilles was on top of him, straddling him with his legs. Cycnus screamed in anger. Achilles tore off his helmet and forced the strap round the Trojan's neck, squeezing with all his strength. While the Greek army forced the Trojans back off the beach to win their first victory, Cycnus groaned and breathed his last.

In the weeks that followed,

Achilles added victory to victory, death to death until his name was the most feared in the entire Greek army. Priam, the King of Troy lost no less than three of his sons to Achilles, his beloved Troilus chased into the temple of Apollo and speared on the very altar itself. With the Myrmidons behind him, Achilles ravaged the countryside, seizing the Trojan herds of cattle and sacking the city of Lyrnessus. It was here that he discovered the beautiful Princess Briseis. Her father had died in the fighting and Achilles, who had fallen in love with her, took her back to his tent to be his serving-maid.

The Wrath of Achilles

It was at this time (in the spring) that Achilles had his second argument with King Agamemnon. They had almost come to blows once when Achilles had suggested that the King of Mycenae had only entered the war out of a sense of guilt and didn't really want to fight at all. Agamemnon had retorted by reminding Achilles of the time he had spent disguised as a girl and after that the two had never been friends.

This new, more serious, argument concerned Briseis. Agamemnon had found himself an equally beautiful captive but had been forced to send her back to Troy when it was discovered that she was a priestess. So now the king seized Briseis for himself, which angered Achilles so much that he stormed off into his tent, refusing to have anything more to do with the war.

At first nobody believed that so great a warrior could behave in such a way, but as the days passed and Achilles failed to appear, they realized he meant just what he said. The Trojans, when their spies reported the news, returned to the battlefield with renewed vigour. This was virtually their first piece of good fortune since the Greeks had landed.

The morale of an army can win a war and suddenly it seemed that the Trojans

had gained the upper hand. A daring sortie was led by Hector, the eldest son of King Priam, and the Greek lines were broken. Both Agamemnon and Odysseus were wounded in the fighting and while the Greeks scattered in panic, Hector pressed on towards their fleet. If he were able to burn their ships and cut the supply lines, he might well end the whole enterprise – but still Achilles refused to fight.

It was Patroclus who saved the day. The flames were already devouring the first ship, black smoke curling up the masts and brilliant sparks cascading on to the water, when Patroclus ran forward, wearing the armour of Achilles, and hurled his spear into the mass of Trojans. He would have been cut down where he stood but for the fact that he so resembled Achilles that the Trojans mistook him for his cousin and fled. Then, while Greek soldiers put out the fire, Patroclus regrouped the rest of the army and chased the fleeing Trojans towards the walls of the city.

Patroclus had lived his whole life in the shadow of Achilles. Where his cousin had been exalted, he had been ignored. Where his cousin was famous, he was unknown. Now, for the first and last time, he found himself the undisputed leader of the suddenly fearless Greek forces and a hero in his own right. He chased the Trojans right back to the walls, while Achilles, hearing what was happening, hastily assembled his Myrmidons. But Patroclus relied on luck as much as skill and now his luck ran out. A chance blow caught him between the shoulder-blades. His helmet was torn off and at the same moment his spear splintered. Blinded, he staggered away from the wall of Troy, then screamed and twisted round as a sword was driven into his chest. Dying, he tried to lift himself out of the mud. That was how Hector found him. One blow and it was over.

When Achilles came upon the body of his cousin, the Greek soldiers were fighting furiously to protect it. With a cry of anger and grief he threw himself into the battle, striking out left and right, forming a bloody circle around the corpse. At last, as the sun was setting, the Trojans retired and Achilles was able to pick up the body of Patroclus and carry it back to the Greek ships that he had saved.

He was buried with full honours beside the sea, the dying sun casting a scarlet banner across the water. Agamemnon, though wounded, came from his tent, bringing Briseis, to make his peace with Achilles. And Achilles, standing beside his cousin's grave, swore revenge on the man who had killed him.

Achilles and Hector

If Achilles was the pride of the Greek army, then Hector was his equivalent in the Trojan. The two men were natural opponents. They were even physical opposites, with Hector's jet-black hair and dark skin. Moreover, although the two had yet to encounter one another on the field, a deep hatred existed between them and each sought revenge on the other, Achilles for the death of Patroclus, Hector for the loss of three brothers, Troilus and Mestor killed and Lycaon captured and sold into slavery for the price of a silver bowl.

Hector had challenged Achilles to single combat once, but that had been at the time when he was refusing to fight. Now he accepted and for one day the war was suspended, both sides standing back to watch the confrontation.

It was a brilliant morning. The waves, hurrying towards the field of combat, seemed to throw precious stones on to the sand as they crashed against the shore. A soft breeze brushed across the Greek camp, tousling the hair of the waiting soldiers. There was a murmur as the gates of Troy swung open and a single figure stepped out, dressed in black and silver armour, a sword in one hand, a spear in the other. Then the flaps of Achilles' tent were pulled back and the murmur became a gasp. Thetis had visited her son that night, bringing with her new armour forged by the immortal Hephaestos himself. Now, as Achilles stood in the sunlight, he seemed to be carved out of solid gold and the reflection of the sun around him was almost blinding.

Perhaps Hector knew at that moment that he was doomed.

Achilles was relentless, unstoppable. Saying nothing, he approached the Trojan, his feet pounding in the dust. As soon as he was within range, Hector hurled his spear. Achilles raised his shield and the spear clattered uselessly to one side. Then Hector ran, not because he was afraid but because he hoped to tire his enemy. Three times he circled the walls of Troy but when he stopped and looked round, Achilles was still the same distance from him, barely out of breath.

Then, with the shouts of the Trojan forces above them and the Greek forces all around them, the two men joined in combat. So ferociously did they fight that when sword struck sword the spark could be seen a mile away. Hector was perhaps the stronger. But Achilles was the faster and, watching from the walls, the Trojans let out a great cry when he dodged one blow, carried his sword in low and ran their prince through the heart.

The Achilles Heel

Hector crumpled to his knees.

'Achilles!' he whispered, the blood curtaining over his lip. 'Let my parents have my body. Let me be buried honourably.'

'Never!' Achilles cried. He twisted his sword and watched the light in Hector's eyes go out.

Then he took the body and, while King Priam looked on, helpless and in horror, he fastened it by the feet to his chariot and rode off around the city. Three more times he circled Troy, dragging Hector behind him. At last he rode back to his camp, taking the body with him. But the ordeal was not yet over for the Trojans. Although they offered their prince's weight in gold for the return of the corpse, Achilles refused. And every day at dawn he would taunt them with it, whipping up his horses around the walls, dragging his enemy in a cloud of dust behind him.

Every day for a week Achilles did the same, deaf to the lamentations of the Trojans and even to the pleas of his own mother. Such was his grief at the loss of Patroclus. At last, the gates of Troy opened and King Priam himself rode out, accompanied only by one young soldier and by four servants carrying a litter. Under the flag of truce, he proceeded to the tent of Achilles and there threw himself on to the ground.

'Achilles!' the old man wept. 'You have proved yourself a great warrior, but have you the compassion to prove yourself a great man? You have killed my eldest child, the son I most loved and in whom I had most pride. What times are these that fine soldiers and princes must perish in the bloom of their

youth! Now, I beg you, show pity to an old man. See – I bring you Hector's weight in gold. Will you not be moved by a father's tears? Think on your own father and let me lay the remains of Troy's noblest prince to rest. Let me bury my son.'

Then Achilles wept too – for his cousin Patroclus, for the futility of war and for the man he had almost become himself. He gave orders for the body of Hector to be carried back to Troy and called for a truce of twelve days in which the funeral solemnities could be prepared.

LEGENDS

The Death of Achilles

The war dragged on. Amongst those who died were, on the Trojan side, Penthesileia, queen of the Amazons and one of the few heroines of mythology, and Memnon, the Ethiopian leader whose skin was as black as ebony and who was said to be the handsomest man alive. The Greeks had their losses too. Antilochus, young, swift and courageous, died at the hand of Memnon, and Thersites, the ugliest soldier at Troy, was actually slain by Achilles himself as the result of an argument.

But for Achilles too, time was drawing in. After the death of Hector, he had fought as bravely as ever, the differences between him and Agamemnon forgotten. On many occasions he routed the Trojans, often coming close to breaching the walls of the city itself. But he had made himself the target of too many enemies, and not all of them were human ones. Poseidon, the

sea-god, still demanded vengeance for the death of his son Cycnus, while Apollo had been enraged by the killing of Troilus which had taken place in his own temple.

So one day in the thick of the fighting, Poseidon whispered to Paris – the man who, more than any other, had begun the

war – that Achilles was not invulnerable, while Apollo guided his hand. For the gods remembered how Thetis had held him when she dipped him in the Styx and now Paris let loose a poisoned arrow which struck him in the heel.

At once Achilles fainted and had to be carried off the field by his Myrmidons. Doctors were called but already the poison had spread through his blood and that night, with Thetis beside him and the stars blazing silver in the sky, he died.

LEGENDS

The Greek army mourned for seventeen days and seventeen nights and the nine Muses themselves came down into the world to sing his dirge. On the eighteenth day his body was burned on a great pyre beside the sea.

And as the smoke rose over the crashing waves, the two armies clashed once again in a war which was tainted by grey despair, a war which was suddenly less glorious and less heroic than it had once seemed.

CATCHING THE SUN

Polynesian

Catching the Sun

To look at, you would not have thought that Maui was a hero. He was very small and very ugly with short, stubby arms and a pot belly. It will come as no surprise to learn that the moment he was born – the fifth of five brothers – his mother picked him up and hurled him into the sea. And yet to the Polynesian people, Maui was one of the greatest if not the greatest of the so-called trickster heroes – which is to say that what he lacked in dignity and grace he made up for in cunning.

He was saved from drowning by his ancestor-in-the-sky, a god called Tama-hui-ki-te-rangi and, dripping wet, with a piece of seaweed dangling behind one ear, made his way to the House of Assembly where his brothers had just been christened. There was a party going on when he arrived, as there is at every Polynesian christening. All the family had been invited and the various relatives were eating their way through baskets piled high with seafood and fruit, drinking exotic cocktails and dancing together under the stars.

This festive atmosphere was abruptly shattered by the appearance of the small and dripping hero.

'Who are you?' his mother demanded.

'I am your son,' Maui replied, rather grumpily.

'Impossible!' the mother sniffed. 'I threw you away the moment you were born.'

'Well I've come back,' Maui retorted. 'And I'd be grateful if you would be so good as to christen me instead of trying to throw me away again.'

Then Maui's father stepped forward.

'How do we know you are who you say you are?' he asked. 'You don't look like your brothers. You could be anybody's child.'

Maui smiled.

'I can prove it,' he said, walking over to where his four brothers were sitting, gurgling like ordinary babies should. 'This one is called Maui-taha,' he continued, pointing. 'This one is Maui-roto. He's Maui-poe. And he's Maui-waho.'

His mother's jaw dropped. 'How do you know?' she asked.

'I spent nine months in the same womb as them,' Maui snapped. 'I ought to have got to know their names!'

When they heard this, his parents were forced to accept that he was their lost son. His father plucked the seaweed off his ear and gave him a towel. His mother apologized for throwing him into the sea. And with the simple name of Maui he was welcomed into the family.

During the next few years, Maui had many adventures. Another ancestor of his – an ancestress, in fact, called Muriranga-whenua – gave him a magic jawbone and he never went anywhere without it. It was by using the magic jawbone that he was able to fish the land of New Zealand out of the sea, although once he had brought it to the surface, his brothers insisted on cutting it up. Naturally they made

a botch job of it and that is why there are so many mountains in New Zealand and so many irregularly shaped islands around it.

Maui's other feats included inventing the kite, the eel-pot and the barbed fishing spears still used by Polynesians to this day. He also single-handedly separated the earth and the sky (which were stuck together at the time), heaving the sky up rather like an Olympic athlete with a dumb-bell. But perhaps his most extraordinary feat, and the subject of this myth, was the catching of the sun.

The adventure began one evening, just as

the sun was setting. He and his brothers had been out fishing but now, as the darkness set in, they were forced to return home. In those days, of course, there was no electricity or gas. The day ended in every sense of the word once it got dark.

'If only the sun stayed up longer,' Maui said, 'we'd all be better off.'

The words were no sooner out of his mouth than he was struck by a thought.

'Hey!' he cried. 'Why don't we catch it?'

His brothers looked at him wearily.

'We couldn't,' one said. 'It's too far away.'

'And too big,' added a second.

'And even if we did catch it,' a third muttered, 'it would only burn us up.'

'It's impossible,' the fourth agreed.

'Nonsense!' Maui shouted. 'You're talking to the man who netted New Zealand and lifted up the sky. Of course we can do it!'

For the next week, the five brothers worked, spinning and twisting ropes to form the noose with which they would catch the sun. The technique they used to make the rope – plaiting the flax into stout, square-shaped lengths – was another invention which you will still find used in Polynesia. It is called tua-maka.

At last, when the rope was ready, they set off. They travelled only at night so that the sun, hidden beneath the horizon, would not see them coming. By day they hid in the desert, sleeping under bushes or covering themselves with a layer of sand. For several months they travelled and in this way they finally arrived at the very eastern edge of the world.

Here, working under Maui's supervision, they built an enormous clay wall with two sheds – one at each end. The sheds were for the four brothers to hide in so that they would not get burned by the sun. The noose was unpacked and dangled over the wall so that it hung in outer space – just underneath the world itself. Maui took his place, standing at the very centre of the world.

And thus prepared, they waited.

Dawn arrived and the unsuspecting sun began its climb.

'It's coming,' Maui whispered, the light dancing in his eyes.

The brothers, hidden in their sheds, tightened their grips on the ends of the ropes.

The sun drew level with the wall.

'Now!' Maui cried, and slipped the noose over it.

At once the sun tried to back away. Brilliant flames exploded around it, tearing at the dark blue fabric of the universe. Burning meteors cascaded down in apocalyptic fury. Had Maui been an ordinary human, he would have been frazzled. But as the furious heat of the sun raced through him, he just laughed and pulled at the rope.

The noose tightened. The sun was caught.

'Now I'll teach you, you old rascal!' Maui giggled.

And, lifting his magic jawbone, he walloped the sun half a dozen times.

'Aaagh!' screamed the sun.

Catching the Sun

'Hold on!' Maui shouted at his brothers, for the ropes were jerking up and down like a snake stew. Again and again he pounded the sun with the jawbone, sparks flying every time it made contact.

'Stop it!' the sun yelled. 'What have I done to you?'

But Maui was beside himself with excitement and didn't listen.

At last he tired of the sport. Climbing back down from the wall, he signalled his brothers who allowed the noose to open again. The sun slipped out and continued its upward climb.

But it was not the same sun that had once circled the earth in seven and a half hours. Now it was bruised, battered and bewildered, quite exhausted by the clobbering it had received at Maui's hands. From that day on, it took twenty four hours to make the round trip – twelve hours from horizon to horizon.

For Maui had not only caught the sun. He'd beaten the living daylight out of it too.

THE GRENDEL

Anglo-Saxon

The Grendel

When King Hrothgar came to the throne of Denmark (in the fifth century after Christ), he decided to build a great banqueting hall in which he would entertain all his friends. And as he was a popular king, who had fought bravely and won many fierce battles, and as he had more friends than most kings tend to have he decided that the hall would have to be larger and more splendid than any in the land of Denmark. This was how Heorot came into being. Heorot the mead-hall, the home of feasting and of singing and of storytelling.

Thatched with heather and decorated by blazing beacons and gilded antlers, the hall would fill every day with warriors and travellers, musicians and poets. King Hrothgar himself would sit at the very end of the hall on a raised dais and sometimes his wife, the fair Queen Wealtheow, would take the seat beside him. The servants would race past the roaring fires carrying steaming plates of eel pie and roasted

boars' flesh to the trestle tables that ran the full length of the room. Hunting dogs, lying on the straw, would raise their heads as the meat went past, their tongues hanging out, and by the end of the feast, they too would have been rewarded with scraps of meat and marrow bones. The mead would never stop flowing. And as the sun reached out to claim possession of the night sky, the music from the harps would still ring out across the fields along with the laughter and the chatter of old comrades at ease.

Grendel heard that sound.

Curled up in the darkness of the swamp, it heard and one poisoned eye flickered open. Softly it growled to itself. For Grendel understood nothing of pleasure and so hated it. Hatred ruled its life. It was descended from Cain – the same Cain that had been cast out of Eden for the murder of his brother. Grendel blamed all mankind for the sin of its ancestor and its own fall from grace. The bitterness of centuries ran in its veins, congealing its blood. In its every waking moment it writhed in a torment of self-pity and half-formed dreams of revenge. Now, hearing the sound, it slithered through the mud and began to limp towards the hall.

It was at that grey time between night and day when it reached Heorot. Now, at last, the revellers were asleep, intoxicated by the wine and good companionship. Grendel struck quickly and greedily. Thirty warriors were snatched up from where they lay. Thirty brave men met a brutal, cowardly death. Glutted with blood, Grendel slunk away, back to the solitude of the swamp. Even in its victory, it knew no pleasure. It had done what it had set out to do; neither more nor less.

The next morning, when King Hrothgar awoke, the sweetness of the banquet turned in an instant to the bitterness of betrayal and death. Blood was everywhere, splattered on the walls and in pools on the flagstones. Nobody had woken up, so stealthily had the Grendel come, and now they found that their clothes were stained with the blood of their friends. Bones and twisted scraps of armour lay on the floor, grim reflections of the debris of the night's feasting. At once a great cry of anger and outrage went up. Spears were seized, swords unsheathed. But it was useless. How could they fight an enemy they could not see – an enemy they had never seen?

Twice more the Grendel came to Heorot, each time returning in the twilight hours to claim another thirty Danish warriors. After that, the hall was closed, and with the booming of the door it was as if all happiness had come to an end in the reign of King Hrothgar. A shadow had fallen not only across Heorot but across the whole country and the emptiness of the banqueting hall soon came to be a fitting image for the hollowness in the heart of all Denmark.

Sometimes, King Hrothgar would return alone to his beloved Heorot. He would sit

on his raised dais, drawing patterns in the dust with one finger. Then he would search with his eyes to see memories of firelight in the darkness and strain with his ears to hear echoes of laughter in the silence. He was an old man now. Twelve whole winters had passed since the Grendel had come to plague him.

It was at Heorot that he met Beowulf.

He was sitting in his chair, muttering to himself, when the door of the banqueting hall crashed open. He squinted as bright sunlight flooded in, capturing a million motes of dust within its golden beams. A figure stepped forward, silhouetted against the light which could almost have been emanating from his own body. The dust formed a shimmering aura around him. The king trembled. Never had he seen a warrior so tall, so strong.

The stranger approached and fell on to one knee. He was dressed in a blue cloak over a silvery mail-shirt. In one

hand he carried a richly decorated shield, in the other a spear. His helmet masked his face but it could not hide the fair hair that tumbled down on to his shoulders nor the bright blue eyes that shone despite the shadows.

'Your majesty!' the figure said.

'Who are you?' Hrothgar demanded, recovering himself.

'My name is Beowulf,' the warrior replied. 'I come from the land of the Geats. I have crossed a great sea to come before you, to serve you. And I do not come alone.'

There was a movement at the door and fourteen more men entered the hall, bringing with them – or so it seemed to the old king – the light that had for so long been absent. As one they knelt before him, forming a semi-circle around his throne.

'We are soldiers of King Hygelac,' Beowulf continued. 'My noble father was Edgetheow, a famous fighter amongst the Geats. I too have found fame in my lifetime, and seek

to add to that fame by destroying the beast
that has emptied this most stately hall. My
own sovereign, ever a friend of the Danes,
bids me wish all health to your majesty. He
too will be glad to see this monster die.'

'Noble Beowulf!' the king replied. 'Well is
your name known to me – and that of your
father. I bid you welcome. But this creature
has already taken ninety of my finest
warriors. I fear your quest is hopeless.'

'Not so!' Beowulf said with a grim smile.
'Tonight, as we feast once again in great
Heorot, I will tell you something of my past
exploits which will remove your fears for
the present.'

And so it was that the servants returned
to Heorot and swept the floors and cleaned
the tables and relit the beacons and fires.
For that one night, Heorot relived its former
glory, only this time it was not Danes who
filled and refilled their goblets, but Geats.
This time the stories were all tales of the
exploits of Beowulf, how he had enslaved

the five giants and destroyed the seething mass of sea-serpents.

'Your monster comes here unarmed,' he told King Hrothgar, 'so unarmed will I fight it. Yes! Neither sword nor spear will I carry. With my bare hands will I fight and defeat the beast.'

The Geats raised their goblets and broke out in song. The notes were carried by the wind away from Heorot, out and across the fields. Fainter now, they travelled over the swamp until at last they reached the lair of the Grendel. Once again, the poisonous yellow eye flickered open. Its brain turned the information over as though it were chewing a piece of meat. Music. Heorot. Man. It reached out with one hand and pulled itself to its feet.

In the banqueting hall, the Geats had finished eating and were lying on their rugs, their eyes closed. Only Beowulf remained half-awake. He had taken off his coat of mail and helmet and given his sword to

his attendant. Unarmed, he lay beside the door, listening to every breath of the wind, to every leaf that rustled on the ground outside.

Gliding through the shadows, the Grendel came. Pushing through the mists that shrouded the moors, it pressed on towards Heorot. When at last it saw the mead-hall, its pace quickened. One scaly foot came down on a twig, snapping it. Beowulf heard the sound and opened his eyes.

The Grendel reached the door of Heorot.

At the touch of its hands, the solid wood crumpled like paper. Two flames ignited in its eyes as it stepped inside, seeing for the first time the fifteen Geats. Saliva dripped from its mouth.

Beowulf had expected it to make straight for him. But one of the young soldiers had chosen to sleep on the other side of the door and it was this unfortunate youth that the monster seized first, tearing him into pieces and swallowing them whole.

Only then, driven to a brutal frenzy by the taste of blood, did the Grendel stretch out its hands and seize Beowulf.

At once it knew that it had made a fatal mistake. Even as its claws tightened, it found itself grasped with a strength that it would have thought impossible in a human. Suddenly afraid, it tried to pull away, to slither back into the darkness in which it had been born, but it was too late. Its whole arm was frozen in Beowulf's grip. Struggle

though it might, it could not escape.

It howled. It howled in terror and sobbed in pain. Hearing the sound, the remaining Geats awoke, reaching for their weapons. But although they could make out the shape of a huge bulk beside the door, it was still too dark to see the Grendel, and when they stabbed at it with their swords, somehow their blades passed straight through it, as if through a shadow.

The Grendel screamed at Beowulf, their heads so close that they almost touched. The monster who had never once in its life known fear had now discovered terror. It had to get away, away from the impossible man who still held it in a savage grip. And away it went – snapping the tendons in its own shoulder, unlocking the bones and tearing the skin. Howling with pain, it fled from Heorot, back into the night, blood gushing from the horrible wound that it had inflicted on itself.

And inside the hall, Beowulf held the

dreadful trophy of his victory. It was the monster's hand, its arm, its entire torn-off shoulder. These he hung beneath the gable of the roof. Heorot was cleansed. Never again would the creature return.

For the Grendel was dying. Even as it fled, sobbing, through the night, its life-blood was flowing out of it. By the time it reached its home in the swamp, it was cold, colder than it had ever been before. Tears flowed from its eyes as it buried its raw, jagged shoulder in the mud, trying to ease the pain.

When dawn finally came it was dead. It had died miserably, alone in its lair, and its soul had been welcomed in Hell.

THE MARES OF DIOMEDES

Greek

The Mares of Diomedes

Hercules, son of Zeus and the mortal Alcmene, was the strongest man who ever lived. It was said that at close range his biceps looked like the Alps and that he could put a man in hospital for six weeks just by shaking hands. You would certainly have been ill-advised to kick sand in the face of Hercules had you seen him at the beach. Not unless you wanted to find yourself several feet under the sand with your legs tied in a knot behind your head.

When Hercules was only a tiny baby, the goddess Hera (ever jealous of her husband's infidelities) sent two enormous snakes to destroy him. Now each snake was several times larger than Hercules, with bulging eyes, ferocious teeth and a spitting, poisonous tongue. But Hercules simply took one in each hand, giggled, and squeezed. And by the time his nurse arrived to see what all the hissing, spitting, giggling and gurgling was about, the baby was sound asleep with two very surprised snakes lying

dead at the bottom of his crib.

Hera, who never forgot a slight no matter how slight it might be, remained his immortal enemy for life and later on succeeded in driving him mad. In his madness, Hercules thought he saw six of his worst enemies and immediately killed them all, only to find that they weren't enemies at all but his own children. For this unfortunate crime, the Oracle at Delphi sent him to Argolis, to work for twelve years under the orders of King

The Mares of Diomedes

Eurystheus. And that is how the famous Twelve Labours of Hercules came about.

Hercules was not at all happy about having to work for a man who, if placed in a boxing ring with him, would have lasted approximately 0.5 of a second. But he could not disobey the Oracle. He was at least well equipped for the labours that would follow. His father, Zeus, gave him an unbreakable shield. The sea-god, Poseidon, gave him a troop of horses. Apollo, god of the sun, gave him a bow and arrows trimmed with eagle feathers. From the messenger-god, Hermes, he received a sword; from Athene, goddess of wisdom, a robe; and from the lame god Hephaestus, a breastplate made of gold. In the next few months, he would need them all.

His first challenge was the Nemean lion, a gigantic, seemingly invincible beast that managed to bite off one of his fingers before he throttled it. Next came the Lernaean Hydra. This was the famous monster with

nine heads that grew two more heads every time one was cut off. In the end, Hercules set fire to the whole lot at once, so destroying it – although he lost part of one toe in the struggle.

Not all the labours involved killing things. The fifth task, for example, was to clean the stables of King Augeias and this could have been the most difficult of all. For the stables were filthy. No fewer than three thousand oxen were kept in them and nobody had been near the place with a mop or a bucket and spade for thirty years. You could smell the Augeian stables from the far side of the Peloponnese and the fields surrounding them for five miles in every direction were not green but brown. As it turned out, much to the annoyance of King Eurystheus, Hercules didn't even get his hands dirty. He simply diverted two rivers into the stables and the rushing waters did all the work for him.

It must be said that King Eurystheus did

not particularly like Hercules. The king was a thin, flabby man who got hay fever in the summer and influenza in the winter. Hercules was massive, in perfect health, the son of a god. And Hercules could crush bricks to powder in his bare hands. King Eurystheus couldn't even grow a decent beard. So the king hoped that Hercules would either fail in one of his labours or, better still, die trying. And with the Mares of Diomedes, he thought he had found a task that would rid the world of the hero once and for all.

'I congratulate you, Hercules,' he said. 'So far you have managed to clean the Augeian Stables. You have killed the Nemean Lion, the Lernaean Hydra and the Stymphalean Birds. And you have captured the Cretan Bull, the Ceryneian Hind and the . . . er . . . Wild Boar of Erymanthus.' He smiled nervously, trying not to remember the wild boar which had frightened him so much at the time that he had dived head-first into a bronze jar and stayed there all afternoon. 'Seven labours well done. Well done indeed!

'I thought for labour number eight, I would give you something a little easier. No monsters this time! No. All I want are the four mares of the Thracian king Diomedes. I'm afraid he's rather attached to them. I understand that he even keeps them in stables made of solid bronze. So I dare say he won't be too happy when you steal them. Still, that should be no problem for a man like you. Or should

I say a demi-god? I mean, you never get hay fever or influenza, do you? You can do anything!'

And with a little chuckle that concealed an unpleasant secret, King Eurystheus climbed down from the throne and went for another – useless – work-out in the palace gymnasium.

Hercules set off at once, travelling with a servant called Abderus. Together, the two men arrived in the Thracian town of Tirida where the four Mares of Diomedes were said to be stabled. All they had to do was to find out where – and this proved no problem as the bronze stables, glinting in the sunlight, could be seen for miles around. What did prove to be a problem, though, was the Bistones.

The Bistones were the soldiers of King Diomedes and a more violent, more bloodthirsty mob would be impossible to imagine. Wherever they went, they were armed to the teeth. In fact even their teeth

The Mares of Diomedes

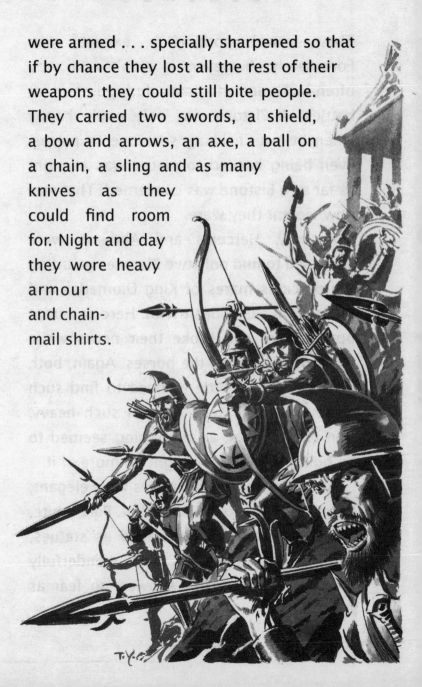

were armed . . . specially sharpened so that if by chance they lost all the rest of their weapons they could still bite people. They carried two swords, a shield, a bow and arrows, an axe, a ball on a chain, a sling and as many knives as they could find room for. Night and day they wore heavy armour and chain-mail shirts.

T·Y·C·

L E G E N D S

They feared nothing – except rust. Fortunately, however, it didn't rain very often in Thrace and never during important battles. A Bistone was only really happy when he was hacking someone to pieces. Even being hacked to pieces was all right as far as a Bistone was concerned. That was how violent they were.

Anyway, Hercules and Abderus were surprised to find only two Bistones guarding the precious mares of King Diomedes and these were easily dealt with. Hercules crept up on them and broke their necks while Abderus unchained the horses. Again, both of them were a little puzzled to find such elegant animals secured with such heavy, iron chains – but as everything seemed to be going well, they thought no more of it.

And the Mares of Diomedes were elegant; there could be no doubt of that. Pure white, they were as perfectly formed as statues, with bright blue eyes and wonderfully untamed manes. They showed no fear as

The Mares of Diomedes

Abderus released them but seemed to lean towards him, nuzzling his collar as he led them out of the stables.

They followed the two men obediently as they left the town of Tirida and made their way towards the coast where the ship was waiting to take them back to Argolis. The only time they showed any fear was when the silence of the late afternoon was shattered by a great cry of outrage. The mares trembled, Abderus went white and even Hercules scratched his head. For the two dead guards and the theft of the horses had been discovered. And right now ten thousand extremely angry Bistones were charging out of the town and up the hillside towards them.

'Abderus! Take the horses!' Hercules commanded. 'Lead them over the brow of the hill and wait for me on the other side.'

'What are you going to do, master?' Abderus cried.

'Don't worry! I've got a plan.'

The Mares of Diomedes

'But there are ten thousand of them!'

'Ten thousand?' Hercules shrugged his shoulders and smiled. 'No problem.'

But even the strength of Hercules might have proved useless against the twenty thousand swords, ten thousand shields . . . and so on of the Bistones, had he not noticed a peculiarity in the landscape on his way to Tirida. The town lay in a deep valley near the coast. The edge of the sea was actually above the town and moreover, there was a single, huge rock lying at the top of the hill between the two of them. All he had to do was to move the stone and the sea would rush along the newly formed channel and down into the valley.

As soon as Abderus and the mares had reached the safety of the shore, he set to work. The stone was vast, ten times his own height and several hundred times his weight. Setting his back against it, he could have been leaning against a small mountain, but he seemed unaware of the challenge.

Closing his eyes and gritting his teeth, the water lapping at his feet, he pushed.

The rock tottered but refused to roll. The Bistones were halfway up the side of the valley now. Already they were shooting off their arrows, the ones at the back accidentally killing the ones at the front in their over-enthusiasm. He pushed again, harder this time. The rock swayed on its base, but still clung to the earth as if glued there. The first Bistone had reached the top of the hill and had drawn both of his swords. Hercules gave a great cry and pushed a third time. Like a loose tooth, the rock finally came free, and as Hercules threw himself out of the way, the waters rushed to fill the hole.

Fifty of the Bistones were crushed by the massive stone as it spun down the hill. Another fifty were killed by their friends as they tried to get out of its way. The rest of them were drowned. The sea exploded through the gap in the hillside, a thousand white horses racing to replace the four that had been stolen. Nothing could stand in its way. Trees were torn out of the ground, houses smashed into a whirling mass of brick and broken wood. In seconds the entire town of Tirida had disappeared underneath a spreading lake, a lake on whose dirty water floated the army of Bistones, swirling round like dead flies.

Meanwhile, on the other side of the hill beside the sea, Abderus was waiting with the horses, quite unaware of what was going on. He was also unaware of something else. For what King Eurystheus had neglected to mention was that the mares of Diomedes were not quite as elegant as they seemed. In fact they were nothing short of monsters, feeding not on hay or on sugar but on the raw flesh of human beings. It had often been a joke of King Diomedes to feed his unsuspecting guests to them. Unfortunately for Abderus, there had not been a guest at the palace for a week.

'Hey – girls – you look hungry,' the servant

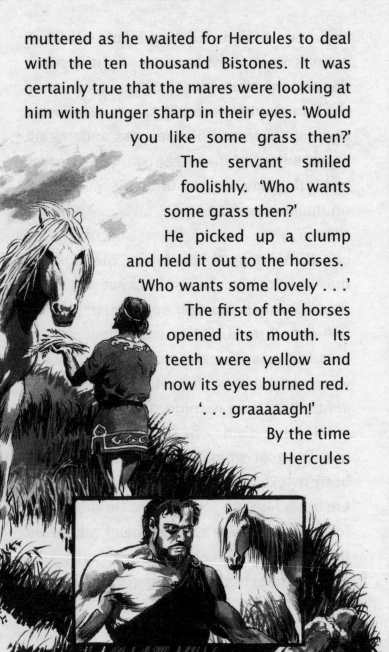

muttered as he waited for Hercules to deal with the ten thousand Bistones. It was certainly true that the mares were looking at him with hunger sharp in their eyes. 'Would you like some grass then?'

The servant smiled foolishly. 'Who wants some grass then?'

He picked up a clump and held it out to the horses. 'Who wants some lovely . . .'

The first of the horses opened its mouth. Its teeth were yellow and now its eyes burned red. '. . . graaaaagh!'

By the time Hercules

returned, there was nothing left of Abderus apart from a few bones, and a little blood flecking the white mouths of the mares. And the four horses were just a little fatter than they had been when he left them. Carefully, he took hold of their chains, understanding now why they needed them. And not once, on the long voyage home, did his eyes leave them.

King Eurystheus was in the bath when he got back to Argolis. The king was in a good mood and had been for some time.

'I expect we'll be hearing about Hercules any day now,' he was saying to the slave who was washing his back. 'I can hardly wait. He'll have beaten the Bistones and stolen the mares – but he'll have never guessed just what he's stolen. Not, that is, until they eat him! Oh dear me yes! That'll teach Mr Muscles.'

The words were no sooner out of his mouth than there was a strange sound from the room next door – a sort of clatter.

'What the . . .?' he began.

And then the four Mares of Diomedes trotted merrily into the bathroom, their hooves striking against the mosaic floor. Eurystheus screamed, swallowed a mouthful of bath water and screamed again.

'Your horses, sire,' Hercules said, walking in behind them.

King Eurystheus had run three and a

half miles before he realized he was still completely naked. And it would be months before he would sleep again without nightmares. The nightmares of Diomedes.

PROCRUSTES AND HIS MAGIC BED

Greek

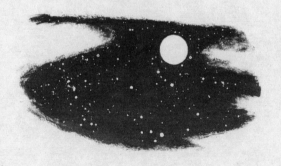

Procrustes and his Magic Bed

Probably one of the most dangerous roads that wound its way through Ancient Greece, or through any other part of the world for that matter, was the coastal road between Troezen and Athens. Certainly no road ever claimed more lives. And yet to look at, it could not have appeared more safe. There were no sharp corners, no crumbling precipices over which an unsuspecting chariot might plummet. The surface was smooth and fairly well maintained. There wasn't even that much traffic, so the chances of a collision or something like that were small.

Why was it, then, that very few of the people who set out from Troezen ever actually arrived at Athens? Why was it that less than half the people leaving Athens ever made it to Troezen?

There were at least five answers to these questions, and none of them were very pleasant ones.

For the road was inhabited along virtually the whole of its length by the most ferocious

Procrustes and his Magic Bed

bandits and the most demented killers you could possibly imagine. There were so many of them that it's amazing that anyone ever dared go that way.

First there was Periphetes who had the charming nickname of the 'cudgel-man', this referring to the enormous club with which he broke travellers' skulls. Then there was Sinis, the pine-bender. He had got into the habit of using bendy pine trees to catapult his victims to their death. Next there was Cercyon, whose hobby was crushing people to death in wrestling bouts, and after him Sciron, who enjoyed kicking passers-by over the edge of a cliff.

But assuming that you hadn't been clubbed, catapulted, crushed or kicked to an early grave, then you might well have met Procrustes. You would soon wish that you hadn't.

Procrustes was the father of Sinis, but unlike the pine-bender, he seemed a kindly, gentle old man, who lived in a beautiful castle just off the road at the top of a hill. You might meet him as you turned a corner and he would smile at you, and the conversation might go something like this:

PROCRUSTES: Good evening!

YOU: Hello!

PROCRUSTES: Travelling far?

YOU: To Athens.

PROCRUSTES: That's quite a way from here. I tell you what – why don't you come back to my castle for a spot of supper? And you can stay the night if you like.

YOU: Well . . . er . . . actually.

At this point you might well hesitate because although the old man smiled very pleasantly and although he didn't look as though he could hurt a fly, he would be surrounded by a number of very large and very ugly men who looked very much as though they could. Some of these would be carrying bows and arrows. Others would be armed with spears or spiked clubs. The rest of them would hold swords, daggers, giant

corkscrews,
iron mallets and
weapons so
peculiarly disgusting
that they didn't even
have names.

And some sixth
sense might
whisper to you
that quite possibly
these people
wouldn't take no
for an answer.

YOU: (Trying to
smile) Well, it's very
kind of you . . .

PROCRUSTES: Not
at all! As a special
treat, you can sleep
in my magic bed.

YOU: Magic bed?

PROCRUSTES: Yes.
I've got this amazing

magic bed. It fits anybody. It doesn't matter how tall you are or how short you are, it's the perfect length for you. Isn't that wonderful?

YOU: Fantastic! Is it comfortable?

PROCRUSTES: It jolly well ought to be. It cost me an arm and a leg . . .

So you would follow the old man into the castle and he would give you an absolutely delicious dinner with plenty of wine and as you grew sleepy you might well think to yourself that you were, after all, really rather lucky to be spending the night in a wonderful magic bed. But you would be wrong. Horribly wrong.

This is how the so-called 'magic' bed worked.

At one end of the bed there was a rope and drum; at the other a razor-sharp cleaver. If you were too short for the bed, Procrustes would stretch you. If you were too long, he would cut off your legs. Either way, it was one bed in which nobody ever woke up.

Only the gods can tell how many

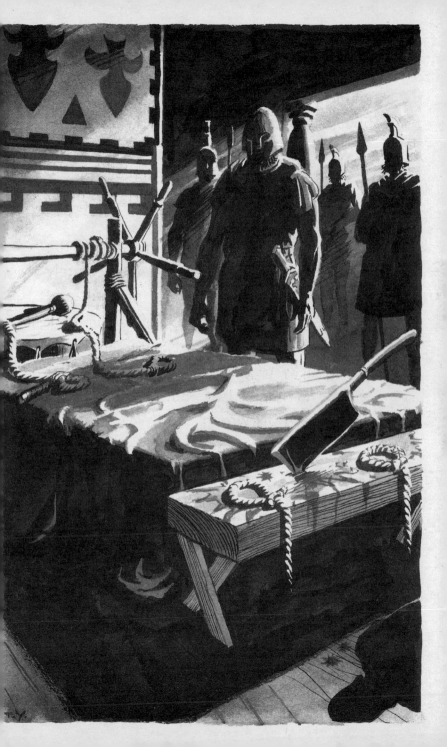

unfortunate travellers Procrustes dealt with in this ghastly manner. He met his own end when the great prince Theseus, son of King Aegeus, travelled along this same road on his way to Athens. It was Theseus who later destroyed the infamous Minotaur – but just to get his hand in, he cudgelled Periphetes, strangled Sinis, broke Cercyon's neck, kicked

Procrustes and his Magic Bed

Sciron over the cliff and finally arrived at the castle of Procrustes.

Procrustes ended up tied to his own bed – although whether he had to be lengthened or shortened nobody knows.

GAWAIN
AND THE
GREEN KNIGHT

English

Gawain and the Green Knight

Part One: The Challenge

It was Christmas at Camelot and for twelve days and nights, King Arthur and his court had been feasting on beef, lamb, pork and chicken, all freshly slaughtered and brought to the table on huge, steaming platters. There were hardly any vegetables . . . it was well known that only poor people ate green vegetables and of course potatoes hadn't been discovered yet. Nor did they eat fresh fruit which was actually thought to be dangerous! No – it was meat, meat and more meat (even the pies contained mince). Washed down with gallons of wine and ale.

As the wind and the darkness swirled around the castle walls, they sat at the table with a huge fire roaring in the hearth and sang or told stories about battles won and dragons slain. More venison! More wine! Outside, the world was cruel and death could strike at any moment. But in Camelot, King Arthur had brought together the greatest and the noblest fighters of his time and bound them together in friendship – the alliance of the Round Table – and for the twelve days of Christmas, nothing was allowed to break the cheerful mood.

However, there was one knight among them who felt less than comfortable, who only reluctantly joined in the singing and had to force himself to laugh at the jokes, particularly the ones that he had heard several times before. His name was Gawain and he was the nephew of King Arthur, a Knight of the Round Table and a man known for his honesty, his good nature and his kindness. You might think that this would be enough for anyone but Gawain had a problem. He didn't feel he was heroic enough.

Gawain was already in his mid-twenties which – at a time when life was short and often ended brutally – was actually quite old. And yet nobody had written any epic poems about him. There were no songs about his exploits. His name was barely mentioned around the fire. The best he had managed so far was to appear in a couple of jokes and even they hadn't been particularly funny. Gawain was a very good-looking young man with light-coloured hair that swept down to his shoulders, blue eyes and a winning smile. He certainly had his fair share of admirers but they were all to be found among the ladies and the maidservants in the castle. But as a warrior he had yet to make his mark.

He had none of the battle scars of old Sir Bors, for example. He couldn't pretend to be as handy with a sword as Sir Percival. And

looking at his two brothers who were sitting on either side of him at the Christmas table, he had to accept that he was in serious danger of being completely forgotten. His older brother, Gareth, for example, had first arrived at Camelot disguised as a servant boy. His adventures in the kitchen had been told and retold a hundred times and there was even a venison stew named after him. The younger brother, Gaheris, had killed so many of his enemies that everyone wanted to be his friend . . . including his enemies who sent him flattering letters and gifts in the hope that he would change his mind about them. Gaheris had once worked for Gawain as his squire-boy. And now Gawain was completely overshadowed. If he hadn't been so noble and generous-hearted, he might have been quite annoyed.

Anyway, he was sitting at the Christmas feast, trying to feel a part of it, when suddenly he heard the sound of approaching hooves. Someone was riding at speed towards the main door of the banqueting hall which seemed like a bad idea because the door was made out of great beams of wood at least nine inches thick and at present it was locked firmly shut. Heads turned. The music stopped. King Arthur himself half rose in his seat, wondering what was about to happen.

And then there was an explosion. The door simply shattered into a thousand fragments as a knight on a horse came smashing through, leaping over the table and coming to a halt on the rush-strewn flagstones in front of the fire. He had brought with him a rush of freezing wind which whipped up the flames, sending smoke and red cinders leaping up the chimney. White steam billowed out of the horse's nostrils and for a moment its eyes seemed to be on fire. Several of the knights had leaped back, their hands on their swords. The servants had scattered. In an instant, everyone in the room was ready for a bloody fight.

The knight was huge. That was Gawain's

first observation. The second was that he – and his horse – were completely green. It wasn't just the great cloak with its fur lining, sweeping over the man's broad shoulders and back. It wasn't just his belt, studded with emeralds, his tunic and his oversized boots. The man's hair and beard were green too. His face was green. His eyes were green. And as the horse threw its head back and whinnied, its green mane seemed to rise up like an ocean wave while its green hooves stamped at the ground and its green tail flicked at the air behind it.

The man was clutching a large bunch of holly in one hand – and that at least was a good omen as holly was often taken as a sign of peace. The other hand was less promising. It held a huge (green) axe at least three feet long, with a razor-sharp blade.

'Who is the master here?' the visitor demanded, his voice ringing out.

At once King Arthur was on his feet. His queen, the beautiful Guinevere, looked on in alarm but knew better than to speak. If there was to be a challenge, if danger and death had come to the castle, it was for the king to deal with.

'I am the one you are looking for,' Arthur replied. His voice was mild. He seemed quite calm about the way the knight had just made his entrance. 'But please – why don't you get down from your horse and join us at our feast? It's Christmas and all are welcome at Camelot.'

'I haven't come to eat with you,' the knight replied. 'But nor am I here to fight you. You may have noticed that I am not wearing my battle helmet and I have brought no weapons.'

'What about the axe?' someone – possibly Gaheris – shouted out.

'The axe?' The giant laughed. 'That's nothing more than a plaything. And, indeed, I have brought it with me because I want to challenge you to a Christmas game. I've heard great things about the so-called Knights of the Round Table. I know how brave you're all meant to be, how noble, how honest. Well, that's what I've come here to witness for myself.'

'What game do you have in mind?' King Arthur demanded.

'Simply this. Whichever one of you accepts this challenge can take my axe and strike me with it. Hit me as hard as you like and wherever you like. I won't move. I won't try to dodge the blow. If you kill me, then so much the better for you. Because there's one catch . . .'

'I knew there'd be a catch,' Sir Bors muttered.

'In one year and one day, the brave knight

must come and accept a blow in return. It's as simple as that. Now – who is it going to be?'

Nobody spoke. Nobody moved. And looking around him, the knight roared with laughter. 'It seems you don't quite live up to your reputations after all!' he exclaimed. 'Is there nobody here bold enough to accept my challenge?'

'We're not silent because we're afraid,' King Arthur assured him. 'It's just that what you suggest is completely monstrous. Why should anyone want to kill you? We don't even know you!'

'Then I will leave and the whole country will know that you failed.'

'I will do the task myself if that's what you really want,' King Arthur said.

'No, my lord . . .'

All eyes turned. Suddenly, Gawain was on his feet. He was completely dwarfed by the green knight who was twice as tall as him and about a hundred pounds heavier. He looked like a boy in front of a man. But even as the challenge had been issued, he had made up his mind. This was the chance he had been looking for.

'Forgive me for speaking without permission.' Gawain went on. 'But this challenge does not seem worthy of a great king. I would like to accept it on your behalf.' He paused for a moment and when nobody interrupted him, he went on. 'The truth of the matter is that my life is worth much less than yours. I've never had a chance to do anything brave or clever. The only thing that's noble about me is that I happen to be related to you. Well, if I may, I'd like to prove myself. I will take up the gentleman's axe and strike him with it. And if by some strange miracle he does survive, then one year and one day from now I will seek him out and accept a blow in return.'

King Arthur considered for a minute. Then he nodded slowly. He understood what his nephew was feeling. 'You have spoken well, Gawain,' he said. 'The challenge is yours.'

Gawain and the Green Knight

'Gawain?' The knight spat out the single word with a sense of mockery. 'Is that your name?'

'It is,' Gawain replied.

'And can you be trusted to keep your word?'

'I am a Knight of the Round Table,' Gawain replied. And for the first time in his life he actually believed it.

'Very well.' The green knight got off his horse and knelt on one knee, holding the axe forward. 'Do your worst – or your best, depending on how you look at it. Remember that in a year from now, you will receive the same in return.'

'Cut well and cut cleanly,' King Arthur advised him. 'But remember . . . only one blow.'

Gawain nodded. His mouth had gone dry. He was aware of all the other knights – and Queen Guinevere – watching him silently. Was this what it was like to be the centre of attention? He could feel his heart beating and his stomach fluttering and knew that he had to control himself. After all, it would do him no good to be seen trembling in front of the whole court. And what exactly was he afraid of? The green knight was kneeling, completely still. He wasn't even going to defend himself. In a minute he would be dead and the challenge would surely die with him. How could Gawain leave in a year and a day to search for a corpse?

He picked up the axe. It was very heavy and the blade dragged across the flagstones making an unpleasant grinding sound. He hoisted it up with both hands. The green knight stayed where he was. Suddenly Gawain wished that he had kept his mouth shut. It wasn't that he was scared. It was just that he was repelled by the idea of striking another man for no reason. And to do so in front of the queen and during the Christmas holidays! It was all wrong.

But it was too late to have any second thoughts. He had accepted the challenge and if he ducked out now, he would never be allowed to forget it. He clenched the axe tighter, the blade high above his shoulder. Then he swung it down.

The metal edge cut through the air and then through the knight's outstretched neck. Gawain felt no resistance at all – not from skin, not from flesh, not from bone. For a brief second, the knight's head remained in place and Gawain felt a bit like a conjuror who had just done a trick – whipping away the tablecloth without disturbing the plates. But then a horrible wound opened up. The head fell to the ground and a huge geyser of blood burst out of the round socket of the neck, reaching almost to the rafters. The blood was red, not green. Some of the knights recoiled in disgust as it splattered down all around.

Gawain waited for the body to topple over. It didn't.

Like something out of his worst nightmare, the knight's arms twitched, then reached forward to pick up the severed head. Holding it by the hair, the body straightened

up, standing in front of Gawain. The head was dangling beside the knight's waist but suddenly its eyes flickered open. They were gazing straight at Gawain.

Then the lips parted and the head spoke.

'You have struck your blow,' the green knight said. 'And a year and a day from now, I will strike mine. But I will make it easier for you to find me. In the land that I come from, I am known as the Knight of the Green Chapel and you can ask for me by that name. Find the green chapel and you will find me.'

The green knight climbed back on to his horse, taking his head with him. The stump of his neck was still bleeding. Blood streamed down his chest and on to the horse's flank. Then his legs kicked back, the horse reared forward and leaped through the shattered doorway. A moment later both of them had gone.

There was a long silence. Then King Arthur stood up again. 'You did well, Gawain,' he said. 'And I know that in a year from now you will live up to your promise. We'll hang the axe on the wall as a reminder of what happened here today.

'And now let's get back to our feasting! It's only proper that you should have a good challenge at Christmas and this was one of the best of all. Servants! Put a heavy curtain over the door to keep the cold out. Wipe up the blood and let's have more wine and more beer and perhaps another roast suckling pig. Minstrels! Let's have another song!'

At once the party began again. Gawain took

his place at the table and his two brothers clapped him on the back, congratulating him on his daring. Up in the gallery, a minstrel had begun a new song:

> *The green knight came – the green*
> *knight said,*
> *'Will someone please chop off my head?'*
> *Gawain the brave, Gawain the true*
> *Took careful aim and cut right through*
> *But now it seems that he is fated –*
> *Soon he'll be decapitated!*

Finally, they were singing about him. But as the wine was poured and more food was served, Gawain found that he had quite lost his appetite and he certainly wasn't going to join in the chorus.

Part Two: The Quest

Slowly and quickly, the year slipped past. To Gawain it sometimes seemed that each day lasted an eternity and yet, when he looked back, six months had passed in the blink of an eye. Meanwhile, life went on as normal all around him. There were jousts and challenges, hunts and banquets. New knights arrived. Old ones took their leave. The truth was that the green knight had almost been forgotten. There were, after all, so many other adventures, so many tales of magic and witchcraft. No one – not even Gawain's brothers – could be expected to think about him all the time.

Finally, on the evening of 1 November, which was also known as All Saints' Day, Gawain knew that it was time to leave. He sought out King Arthur and, bowing low, asked his permission to set off on the quest as he had promised almost a year before.

King Arthur looked at him a little sadly. He didn't expect he would ever see Gawain again. 'Of course you must go, my boy,' he muttered. 'You must be true to your word. And I wish you good fortune in the days ahead.'

Gawain swallowed. He wished the king hadn't used the word 'ahead'.

Sir Bors, Sir Percival, Gareth and Gaheris all turned out to watch Gawain leave. His armour had been set out on a rug and they helped him fasten the different pieces until he looked like a metallic man, glittering in the early winter sun. Finally, he picked up his shield which was bright red with a golden, five-pointed star. The star was known as the Endless Knot and it was a symbol of trust. The four men clapped him on the back and walked out with him to where his horse, Gringolet, was waiting. Gawain mounted and with a final farewell rode away from Camelot. The four men watched him until he had become a speck on the horizon. Then

they turned round and went back in for lunch.

And so began the long journey across the great wilderness of ancient Britain. Gawain started by crossing the northern parts of Wales. He passed the Isles of Anglesey and skirted round Holyhead. He followed the edge of the Forest of Wirral, not daring to lose himself in the wild labyrinth of trees. He and Gringolet clambered up mountains and sank into deep valleys and everywhere they went they searched for the green

chapel and the knight who might live there. They met farmers and blacksmiths and gypsies and wandering troubadours and adventurers but nobody could help them. Time was running out and, worse still, it was getting colder and colder as the full force of winter arrived. Soon it was snowing and the whole landscape was dusted white. At night, Gawain lit a fire and curled up next to Gringolet with the same blanket covering them both. By morning, they could barely move and it took them an hour to force some feeling into their frozen limbs.

November turned into December and as the last month of the year drew to a close, Gawain began to fear that he would break his promise after all. He couldn't find the green knight and his strength was beginning to fail. Christmas Day had come and gone without his even noticing. One night it snowed so hard that in the morning he found himself completely buried and that was when his resolve almost broke. He would have wept but for the fact that his tears would have frozen on his cheeks. Instead, he prayed for help, resting on his knees with his head bowed. Gawain had always been a religious man. But these were prayers uttered without hope. He really thought his life was over.

He pressed on and as the sun began to set, early in the afternoon, he climbed the brow of a hill and saw, in front of him, a huge castle. It really was a miracle. There were no other buildings around. He hadn't spoken to anyone for days. But here was a construction that almost compared with Camelot, with soaring towers and battlements, a fine portcullis, smoking chimneys and thatched roofs. He could only begin to guess at the life that must be teeming inside – torches blazing on the walls, musicians playing, huntsmen, falconers, pages and esquires all bustling together, going about their business, hardly aware of the harsh winter climate beyond the solid walls.

But would they let him in? Approaching a strange castle in these ancient times was always a risk. You were as likely to get a javelin through your chest or a cauldron of boiling oil over your head as a friendly welcome and an invitation to dinner. Still,

Gawain knew he had no choice. He would not survive another night out in the open and so, spurring Gringolet on, he crossed the moat (fortunately the drawbridge was down) and rang the main bell.

A moment later, the door opened and a porter appeared. He looked out suspiciously. But at least he didn't seem completely hostile.

'Good evening,' Gawain gasped. His breath came out in a frosty cloud. 'I'm lost and I'm cold. I wonder if you would let me stay here for a night or two? My name is Gawain. I come from the court of King Arthur and I'm in need of warmth and a little comfort.'

'You've come to the right place!' the porter exclaimed, cheerfully. 'Come in! Come in! You and your fine horse are equally welcome.'

Gawain found himself being led into a magnificent place – better even than he had imagined. A groom hurried forward to look after his horse and he himself was taken to a handsome bedroom with a fire blazing in the hearth and a king-sized bed with woollen blankets and a mattress stuffed with fresh straw. Two servants helped him out of his armour and stood over him as he washed in a hot tub (a real luxury at a time when people only bathed about once a month). Fresh clothes had been provided for him including an embroidered silk cloak with a fur collar that was actually rather grander than anything he himself owned.

At last he was taken down to the main hall where a broad-shouldered, bearded man stood waiting for him at the head of the table. It was obvious from his lavish clothes, his many jewels and from the way the crowd stood silent and watchful in his presence, that this was the lord of the castle. But it was his wife who caught Gawain's eye. She was incredibly beautiful. She reminded him a little of Queen Guinevere, with long, fair hair, a slender neck, very pale skin and perhaps just a glint of mischief in her eyes. She was wearing a flowing silk dress, a fabulous pearl necklace and the rings on her fingers sparkled, each one a different colour. Gawain had to force himself to take his eyes off her and turn them instead to his host.

'So you are Gawain!' the lord exclaimed. He had a voice that was used to making itself heard all around the castle. 'And you come from the court of King Arthur. I've heard many wonderful stories about Camelot and it is a pleasure to meet you. My name is Bertilak de Hautdesert and I am the master of this place. I hope you will join us for dinner tonight and stay with us because this is still Christmas time and we have a week of feasting ahead of us.'

'I thank you for your hospitality,' Gawain replied. 'And I will be glad to stay with you tonight. But tomorrow I must be on my way.' As he spoke the words he looked so downcast that many of the lords and ladies muttered amongst themselves, knowing that something must be wrong.

'Why such a hurry?' Bertilak demanded.

Gawain and the Green Knight

'Do you not have feasts and celebrations at Camelot?'

'Indeed we do,' Gawain replied. He couldn't help remembering that it was at a feast just like this, almost exactly a year ago, that his ordeal had begun. 'But I have made a pledge. In just four days I have to show myself at the chapel of the green knight. I've been looking for it for weeks and I still have no idea where it is. I'm glad to take shelter with you but I dare not stay one minute longer than I have to. This chapel could be many miles away . . .'

At this, Bertilak roared with laughter. 'The chapel of the green knight is just down the road!' he cried. 'I know it well. It's about a mile and a half from the front door as the crow flies . . . not that you get many crows around here. The green knight's scared them all away! I shudder to think what business you have with him and I won't ask. But whatever it is, you can rest and relax in our company. And now . . . let's eat!'

Everyone cheered when they heard this. Bertilak sat him down at the table and Gawain saw that Lady Bertilak had taken the place on his other side. He hardly dared look at her. Her beauty took his breath away and he knew that there was no worse crime than to desire another man's wife. It was a particularly bad idea when that man was his host and in charge of a court that would tear him to pieces if he stepped out of line.

The food was served and for a brief time Gawain was able to imagine that he was back in Camelot at another Christmas feast before the green knight had ever made his unwanted appearance. As the wine was poured and the main course (an entire cow) was sliced, Lord Bertilak leaned over and addressed him.

'We'll be going out hunting tomorrow,' he said. 'Would you like to come?'

'You're very kind, my lord,' Gawain replied. 'But in all honesty, I'm exhausted from my long journey—'

'Leave him behind!' Lady Bertilak exclaimed. 'You can see how tired he is. And from the sound of it, he has quite an ordeal ahead of him. He needs to recover his strength.'

'Very well,' Bertilak said. Then a thought seemed to occur to him and he smiled as he turned to Gawain. 'I'll tell you what,' he went on. 'As this is Christmas, I'd like to play a game with you. Let's make a pledge with each other. I will give you everything we capture or kill on our hunt tomorrow. But in return, you must give me everything you receive while you are in my castle. You must leave nothing out – and nor will I. What do you say?'

In truth, the game sounded rather strange to Gawain. He also remembered that it was a similar sort of game – a blow for a blow – that had led to all this trouble in the first place. But of course, a thousand years ago people entertained themselves in all sorts of peculiar ways and anyway Gawain was far too polite to refuse.

'I'm not sure I'll get anything you want,' he said. 'But if it amuses you to make this pledge, then of course I agree.'

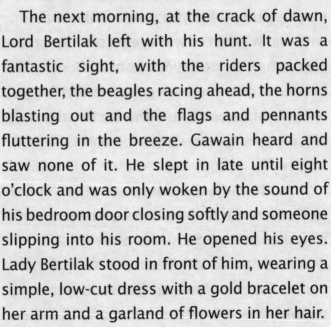

'Everything?'

'Everything!'

And the two of them shook on it.

The next morning, at the crack of dawn, Lord Bertilak left with his hunt. It was a fantastic sight, with the riders packed together, the beagles racing ahead, the horns blasting out and the flags and pennants fluttering in the breeze. Gawain heard and saw none of it. He slept in late until eight o'clock and was only woken by the sound of his bedroom door closing softly and someone slipping into his room. He opened his eyes. Lady Bertilak stood in front of him, wearing a simple, low-cut dress with a gold bracelet on her arm and a garland of flowers in her hair.

She sat down on the bed. 'Good morning,

my lord,' she said.

'Hello!' Gawain wasn't at all sure what to say. He wasn't used to strange women walking into his bedroom first thing in the morning, and there was something about the way Lady Bertilak was looking at him that brought the blood rushing to his cheeks. She leaned over him, her long hair brushing against his face. Gawain reached for the covers and pulled them up to his neck.

'I just wondered if there was anything you wanted to do today?' she asked. Her voice sounded innocent. Her eyes were anything but.

'No!' Gawain managed a one-word answer. It came out strangely high-pitched.

'There's nobody around,' the lady said. 'My husband has gone on his hunt. The servants and my handmaidens are still asleep. And –' she giggled quietly – 'the door is locked.'

'I don't think it is,' Gawain muttered.

'Oh yes it is. I locked it on the way in.'

'Well . . . I . . . I'm . . .' Gawain didn't know what to say. Of course, he was horribly tempted to take this beautiful woman in his arms. But all the laws of courtesy and hospitality forbade it. On the other hand (he told himself) who could possibly find out what happened in the privacy of this room? 'I really am very tired,' he finally exclaimed. 'I'm afraid I must ask your ladyship to leave.'

'Are you sure?'

'Absolutely!'

'Very well. But before I go, I'm sure you won't mind if I give you a kiss.'

'A kiss?'

'Just one kiss. A little something to remember me by.'

'Well . . . if you really insist . . .'

What was wrong with a single kiss? Gawain closed his eyes and a moment later he felt the lady's lips, soft and comforting, against his. He smelled lavender oil on her skin. He felt the weight of her body pressing down on his chest. And then, with a swirl of silk, she was gone. Gawain felt his heart pounding. He didn't dare open his eyes until he had heard the door open and close. When he finally looked, he was alone.

That night, Lord Bertilak came roaring into the great hall with his falconers and stable boys, his archers, his foresters and friends. They were all sweating and covered in mud. They'd had a successful day and there would be meat for everyone that night. Gawain was waiting for him and Bertilak rushed up to him and swept him into a powerful embrace.

'We took a deer!' he shouted and everyone around him burst into applause. 'It tried to escape us but the hounds brought it down and the archers finished it off. Here it is!' The dead animal was tied by its feet, dangling from a long stake which was being carried by six serving boys. 'It is yours, Gawain!' Bertilak said. 'You see how I keep my promise? Now what have you got for me?'

'I'm afraid I got rather less than this magnificent deer,' Gawain replied. 'But everything I received I will give to you, as we agreed.' And with that, he leaned forward and kissed Bertilak full on the lips.

There was a deathly silence. One of the minstrels dropped his lute and it fell to the stone floor with a twang. Nobody spoke. They couldn't believe what they had just seen. And how would Bertilak respond? If he took out his sword and plunged it into his guest, nobody would be remotely surprised.

But then Bertilak roared with laughter and immediately everyone relaxed and began to laugh too. The foresters applauded. A couple of falconers kissed each other just to show that they were in on the joke. 'That is well done, Gawain!' Bertilak cried. 'And we will do the same tomorrow and the day after. Let us hope that whoever gave you this sweet kiss will return and give you another.'

Well, the same thing did happen the next day. The hunt left at dawn and Gawain woke to find Lady Bertilak once more back in his chamber. It seemed to him though that this time her dress was a little shorter and her figure was even more shapely. And this time, she wasn't content to leave him with a single kiss. She insisted on giving him two.

And that night, Lord Bertilak and his men charged in with a huge boar which the chefs could hardly wait to roast and serve with two gallons of apple sauce. But first, as he had promised, the master of the hunt bowed and presented it to Gawain. And Gawain responded by embracing him and kissing him twice – much to the delight and merriment of the court.

By now the green knight had been completely forgotten. As he went to bed that night, all Gawain could think about was the visit from Lady Bertilak that would take place as soon as the sun had risen. Part of him wished that she would stay well away. But part of him looked forward to the kisses and wondered if he would be able to resist if she offered him more.

He was awake early the next morning and this time he heard the hunt leave. At once, the door opened and Lady Bertilak came gliding over to the bed. 'What would you like from me today, Gawain?' she asked.

'I will take whatever your ladyship is pleased to give me,' Gawain replied.

'Well, I have something very special for you. It is something which I think you need.' And having said this, she produced a piece of green material which looked like a belt but which was softer and wider. 'This is a girdle,' she explained. A girdle was a sort of loincloth. It was worn by men and by women underneath their clothes. Many people thought it would help to protect them. 'It's a magic girdle,' she went on. 'If you wear it, nobody will be able to hurt you. It doesn't matter how hard they strike you nor what weapon they use. You will feel no pain and you will not be killed. It is my gift to you, Gawain, a souvenir of your visit to this castle. Keep it close to you and use it well!'

Then she kissed him three times and with a look full of sadness and regret, she stood up and left the room.

Gawain lay where he was, clutching the green girdle in both hands. He couldn't believe what had just happened. The next day he was going to leave the castle and travel to the chapel of the green knight. He was going to stand there, motionless, not putting up any fight or resistance as his head was chopped off. For a whole year he had been dreading it. And now, at the very last moment, he had been given the one thing that might save him!

But what of his promise to Lord Bertilak?

That night, the hunt brought in a handsome fox. It was no good for the pot but its pelt would make someone a fine neck warmer or hat. As usual, Lord Bertilak presented it to Gawain. 'This is all we got!' he explained. 'But as we agreed, it is yours. Now. What have you got for me?'

Gawain gripped his host between his hands and planted three firm kisses on his cheeks. The crowd howled and applauded. Lord Bertilak grinned and shook his head.

'Three kisses!' he boomed. 'Every day it gets better and better. But tell me, my friend, is that all you received today?'

Was there something in his voice? And in his eyes? Could it be possible that he knew?

Gawain held his ground. 'Yes, my lord,' he said. 'I'm sorry I have nothing more to offer you in return for this fine fox.'

The green girdle was in his room, upstairs. He couldn't hand it over, not when his entire life depended on it. But even as Gawain took his place at the table and the next banquet began, he felt uncomfortable. He had behaved dishonourably. He might have saved his own life but what exactly was that worth when he knew he would always have to live with the shame of what he had done?

Part Three: The Green Knight

Gawain left early the next morning, saddling Gringolet and slipping away before anyone was up. It had snowed heavily during the night and the whole landscape was strangely silent, the trees heavy, everything still. The horse's hooves disappeared into the thick layer of white powder that covered the ground, leaving a series of dark holes, each one perfectly spaced. Nobody had been out yet. If anyone had decided to follow Gawain, it would have been a simple task.

Lord Bertilak had shown him the direction in which the green chapel lay and he had ridden for less than an hour before he found it. In this great, white emptiness, it could be seen a mile away . . . a round, stone building surrounded by a clump of dead trees, their black branches stretching out as if to embrace it and keep it a secret to

themselves. There was a horse tethered outside, its nostrils steaming in the cold air, and Gawain recognized it at once. How could he not? It was a brilliant green.

Gawain brought Gringolet to a halt and dismounted. Part of him was afraid. Part of him knew that so long as he carried the green girdle, he could not be hurt. He tied the horse and pushed his way through the snow, making for the chapel. An arched wooden door with a great steel ring led in. He pushed the door. It opened.

The green knight was waiting for him inside, standing in a shaft of light that slanted down from a window above the altar. He was leaning on his axe which he held in front of him with both hands, the blade resting on the floor. This time he wore his helmet. As the door swung open, his head turned slowly and Gawain almost heard the different parts of his armour grinding against each other.

'So you came,' he said.

'I came,' Gawain replied.

'A year and a day ago you struck at me and now it is my turn to do the same. Remember – you cannot defend yourself. You cannot even move.'

'I know the rules,' Gawain muttered.

'Then let's get this business over with.'

Gawain stepped forward and knelt in front of the green knight. Out of the corner of his eye, he saw the huge axe rise up as the knight lifted it effortlessly. There was a cross on the altar and he wished he'd thought to say a quick prayer before he surrendered himself. But it was too late now. And surely there was no need for prayer! He was wearing the girdle. He was protected.

The axe flashed down. At the last minute, Gawain jerked backwards and the blade swept past harmlessly. It wasn't that he was scared. He just couldn't help himself. It was against every human instinct to allow himself to be killed, to have his head lopped off his shoulders. For that was surely what would have happened.

That had been the knight's aim.

'You cheated!' the green knight roared. 'You moved!'

'I'm sorry.' Gawain was close to tears. His behaviour had been inexcusable. If King Arthur and the Knights of the Round Table had been watching, they would have been shocked. 'Try again!' he insisted. 'This time I will be still.'

The green knight lifted the axe a second time. Gawain clasped his hands in front of him, willing himself to be still. He thought about the girdle. He could feel it against his skin. The girdle

would protect him . . .

But what if Lady Bertilak had been lying? What if she was wrong?

The axe sliced through the air. Once again, Gawain pulled back. He saw the sharpened edge pass in front of him, half an inch from his throat. He even felt the cold breeze whipping across his skin.

'Forgive me!' he cried, before the green knight could say anything. 'Try a third time, great knight. And this time, I swear by all that is most holy, I will not move. This time your blade can do its worst.'

'Do not disappoint me, Gawain,' the green knight murmured. 'I am beginning to think that all the stories I have heard about you and your friends at Camelot are just fairy tales.'

'I am ready for you,' Gawain said. 'Speak no more.'

And he was ready. A great calm had come over him. Maybe the girdle would protect him and maybe it wouldn't but he no longer cared. He wasn't afraid of dying. How could he possibly be and remain a Knight of the Round Table?

The green knight took aim one last time. The blade came scything down. And this time Gawain stayed completely still.

But the axe didn't kill him. It didn't cut off his head. Instead, it nicked the side of his neck as it swept past. Blood spurted out. Gawain gasped and clamped a hand on to the wound. At that moment, he knew that the girdle hadn't worked – that it would never have worked. Lady Bertilak had told him that if he wore it, he would feel no pain. But his neck was on fire. Blood was still trickling between his fingers.

Had the green knight missed? That was his first thought. But somehow he knew that his life had been spared on purpose . . . that his opponent had been planning this all along.

'And so the business between us is finally over,' the green knight said. He put down the axe and then lifted off his helmet.

Gawain and the Green Knight

Gawain was astonished to find himself staring at Lord Bertilak.

His host of the night before was no longer green beneath the armour and nor was he angry or threatening. 'I'm sure you want an explanation for everything that has happened,' he began. 'And I will tell you at once. Don't be angry, Gawain, but the entire challenge – my visit to Camelot last year and your recent experiences at my castle – were all a test, put together by a certain lady who goes by the name of Morgan Le Fay.'

At once, Gawain began to understand. Morgan Le Fay was a powerful sorceress who lived in the woods close to Camelot. Some said that she was the daughter of Arthur's mother and therefore half-sister to the king. But nobody was quite sure who she was and they couldn't even say for certain whether she was a friend or an enemy. It was quite possible she was both.

'It was a test of your honesty, your courage and chivalry,' Bertilak continued. 'Would you seek me out as you had promised and would you remain motionless to receive the blow that you thought would kill you?'

'What about your wife . . .?' Gawain stammered. His whole mind was in a whirl. For a whole year he had been living with the knowledge of his certain death. And now . . .?

'My wife was part of it,' Bertilak replied. 'I know that she came to your room three times and I know you resisted her advances. You were completely true to your word, Gawain – except in one respect. We promised we would give each other everything we received over the period of three days and I gave you the deer, the boar and the fox that we took on our hunts. In return, you gave me the kisses that my wife had bestowed upon you – one on the first night, two on the second and three on the third. But at the very end you kept something back . . .'

'The girdle.' Gawain bowed his head.

'Exactly. And that is why the edge of my blade wounded you. It was a punishment for your breach of trust and the scar will always be a reminder to you. But now the test is over. You have acquitted yourself like a hero, Gawain. Come! Take my hand. I hope there is no bad blood between us.'

Gawain shook Bertilak's hand but after he had left the chapel, he did not return to the knight's castle, not even to say a final goodbye to Lady Bertilak. The truth was that he was anxious to be away, to get back to Camelot. He knew that the journey would take him several days and he couldn't wait to be back at the fireside with his brothers and friends.

And as he rode across the snow-driven plains, he wondered what everyone would make of his adventure. Had it really been an adventure at all? After all, the green knight had never existed. The green girdle hadn't been magical. It wasn't as if he had slain a powerful dragon or fought in mortal combat with an equal wizard. 'It was a test . . .' Bertilak's words haunted him as he rode silently on. And in a sense he had failed. By keeping the

LEGENDS

girdle, he had shown himself to be less than one hundred per cent true. Gawain felt down-hearted. He was certain that nobody would ever celebrate his exploits. There would, after all, be no more songs.

But in this he was wrong. 'Gawain and the Green Knight' became one of the most celebrated tales of ancient Britain. When King Arthur heard what had happened, he ordered all the Knights of the Round Table to wear a green girdle in order to remind them that nobody is perfect – and that to believe otherwise is to make a potentially dangerous mistake. So in the end, Gawain got his wish. He heard the minstrels celebrate his adventure and it might have pleased him to know that hundreds of years later, in the fourteenth century, he would become the subject of a great poem. More recently, the story of Gawain and the Green Knight has been turned into a film, a play and even an opera. The most recent version, as far as I know, is this one – and it's fairly certain that it won't be the last.